Critical acclaim for THE EFFECT OF GAMMA
RAYS ON MAN-IN-THE-MOON MARIGOLDS.

Winner of the Pulitzer Prize for Drama
Winner of the Drama Desk Critics Circle award
An ALA Best Book for Young Adults

"Paul Zindel has written a masterful, pacesetting drama. It combines moments of pain, poignancy, beauty, and hope. It is the most compelling work of its kind since Tennessee Williams' *The Glass Menagerie*."—*VARIETY*

"The ultimate accolade must go to Paul Zindel for creating a psychologically perceptive ambience. Shame hangs in the air of this house as palpably as poison gas. And yet, Zindel reminds us, strong, strange, beautiful flowers spring from such compost heaps. It is a troubling thought, one of the honest and intelligent values of this splendid and tormented play."—*TIME*

Books by PAUL ZINDEL

The Gadget

The Pigman

My Darling, My Hamburger

I Never Loved Your Mind

The Effect of Gamma Rays on Man-in-the-Moon Marigolds
(Winner of the Pulitzer Prize)

Pardon Me, You're Stepping on My Eyeball!

Confessions of a Teenage Baboon

The Undertaker's Gone Bananas

The Pigman's Legacy

A Star for the Latecomer (with Bonnie Zindel)

The Girl Who Wanted a Boy

Harry and Hortense at Hormone High

To Take a Dare (with Crescent Dragonwagon)

The Amazing and Death-Defying Diary of Eugene Dingman

A Begonia for Miss Applebaum

The Pigman & Me

David & Della

Loch

The Doom Stone

Reef of Death

Raptor

Rats

The Gadget

Night of the Bat

THE EFFECT OF GAMMA RAYS ON MAN-IN-THE-MOON MARIGOLDS

A DRAMA IN TWO ACTS

by PAUL ZINDEL

🔥 HarperTrophy®
An Imprint of HarperCollins*Publishers*

The Effect of Gamma Rays on Man-in-the-Moon Marigolds
Copyright © 1970, 1971 by Paul Zindel
Copyright © 2005 by Paul Zindel Trusts

Library of Congress Cataloging-in-Publication Data
Zindel, Paul.
The effect of gamma rays on man-in-the-moon marigolds ; a drama in two acts.
p. cm.
ISBN 0-06-075738-8 (pbk.)
PS3576.I518 E3 1971   72177039
[Fic]   CIP
                                                                              AC

Typography by Larissa Lawrynenko
❖
Originally published by Dramatists Play Service October 1970
Included in a Dodd, Mead anthology November 1970
Trade edition published December 1970
First Harper Trophy edition, 2005
Visit us on the World Wide Web!
www.harperteen.com

13 14 15 16 OPM 20 19 18 17 16 15 14 13 12

To Betty Frank

MARIGOLDS . . . REVISITED

It's been many years since my autobiographical play *The Effect of Gamma Rays on Man-in-the-Moon Marigolds* opened Off Broadway and won the 1971 Pulitzer Prize for drama. I can't help being reminded of my favorite theory: We all, most basically, create and tell stories to solve problems. We conjure all sorts of strange characters, march them into frantic conflict with each other, and, at the end of the battle, hope we've learned something. It's important, too, that those who read and hear our stories find answers for their own lives. We look for insights, epiphanies, that shed light on humanness, tolerance, anguish, and compassion. We want to glimpse who we really are and understand why we're on this planet. And, of course, we writers write in dreamlike codes, do anything to throw our readers off the track, praying no one will catch on that we are putting on display little pieces of our joys, our fears, and our hearts.

I used whole chunks of my mother to create the character of Beatrice, the disturbing, manless mother who struggles to make it through life and a science fair with a couple of teenagers. Smaller pieces of my older sister, Betty, were used to create the nightmare-ridden, epileptic Ruth. I wrote my sister's pet rabbit into the drama, along with the single, spectacular convulsion Betty experienced when she began her teen years. And I gave Ruth my sister's incipient puberty, made a torment by my mother's belief that boys and men mustn't be trusted.

I sketched a speck of myself into *Marigolds*, changing my sex to become the fictional, life-affirming Tillie. And the lesson I learned by writing the play with thoughtfulness, honesty, amazement, and terror was that youth is resilient in the clutch of darkness. Between the lines was a love letter to my teachers and librarians and the entire public school system, the world that had been my, and my sister's, salvation from the madhouse.

In the summer of 1996, more than a quarter of a century after audiences and critics had praised *Marigolds*, I traveled to Dorset, Vermont, to see a splendid, daring production of the play. I couldn't help wondering what my story would hold for me after all that time. I had suspected that the triumph of youth would still be vital, emotional, and extraordinary. But would my long-ago-conceived characters, struggling for their dreams in that small, ancient Staten Island store, hold any new answers for me?

They did.

For me, the play continued to resonate on many levels. There was the unspoken, the personal, in which my sister had always been my historian and guide. Betty reminded me how lucky we had felt as children that there was a World War II: We could always explain our missing father by saying he was away fighting the enemy. The truth was that he was a policeman in Manhattan; he had a girlfriend and no time for us. When the war was over, we told everyone our father had to stay overseas an extra two years on a highly classified assignment with the army. Ultimately, the fib bought us a seven-year excuse for why we had no father.

Being fatherless was difficult in the not-so-good old days. Betty and I were scorned, ridiculed, by other kids. If we accidentally broke a window, people would say it was because we were fatherless, that we were poorly brought up. Society was even harder on my mother for having no husband, and it helped to mold her into an eccentric, shrill woman who was frightened of the world. In retrospect, I understand that my sister and I were the ones who saw things as they were, not our mother. She had movielike dreams. She devoured glamorous ads and always said, between suicide threats, that things were getting better. She'd say that one day we'd have our own warm brick home and a new General Motors car and a *House Beautiful* garden filled with American Beauty roses and lilies of the valley. My sister would always ask, "When, Mom? When?"

And while our mother dreamed and held on to a

bizarre, preposterous pride, some nights there would be no food to eat, no coal to burn. She forced us to live in a secret poverty. *Keep your feet down in public or people will see you have holes in your shoes. No, you can't go to church because you have no decent clothes. People will talk about you.* When Sunday came, she'd make us draw the shades and hide in our wreck of a house.

She had had a strange childhood herself. Her mother died when she was a kid. She was spoiled by her father, who would pay "normal families" to take her in and care for her. He slaved on his vegetable wagon to buy her fur-trimmed coats and silk underwear. There was no one who dared to teach her reality. Children of relatives hated her because they had to wear her castoffs. Ultimately, she learned from the street.

She threw temper tantrums. Once, she set her aunt's garage on fire because her aunt had disciplined her. Our mother was a high-school dropout who married the class football hero. And Paul Zindel, Sr., was another dreamer. They were two dreamers who had children.

Now, as I returned to the play more than twenty-five years after its first production, I found questions lurking in the shadows of Beatrice Hunsdorfer's vegetable store that I hadn't even known I'd asked. What is it, really, to grow up in a home without a loving, competent father or mother? Do we yet understand the pain and loneliness and disability of kids who do? And from where do survivors of such homes conjure the magic to insist that, despite everything, their dreams will stay alive?

In the long-vaporized world in which the strange Zindel trio lived, I glimpsed a valor and pluck that are often now part and parcel of young people. Most teenagers today don't allow themselves to be profaned in silence. They refuse to allow anyone to pull down the shades and make them hide. They often shout with a startling honesty that signals that the humanness of all of us has crept boldly forward. I cheered recently when a kid I met told me matter-of-factly in front of his class:

"Three of my parents are media specialists."

The EFFECT
of GAMMA RAYS on
MAN-in-the-MOON
MARIGOLDS

Characters

TILLIE:
The Girl

"In front of my eyes, one part of the world was becoming another. Atoms exploding . . . atom after atom breaking down into something new . . . It would go on for millions of years . . ."

BEATRICE:
The Mother

"This long street, with all the doors of the houses shut and everything crowded next to each other . . . And then I start getting afraid that the vegetables are going to spoil . . . and that nobody's going to buy anything . . ."

RUTH:
The Other Daughter

"Well, they say I came out of my room . . . and I started down the stairs, step by step . . . and I heard the choking and banging on the bed . . ."

NANNY

. . .

JANICE VICKERY

. . .

THE SETTING

A room of wood which was once a vegetable store—
and a point of debarkation for a horse-drawn wagon
to bring its wares to a small town.

But the store is gone, and a widow of confusion
has placed her touch on everything. A door to
NANNY'S room leads off from this main room, and in
front of the door hang faded curtains which allow
ventilation in the summer. There is a hallway and a
telephone. A heavy wood staircase leads to a landing
with a balustrade, two doors, and a short hall.
BEATRICE sleeps in one room; TILLIE and RUTH
share the other.

Objects which respectable people usually hide in
closets are scattered about the main room: newspapers, magazines, dishes; empty bottles; clothes; suit-
cases; last week's sheets. Such carelessness is the type
which is so perfected it must have evolved from
hereditary processes; but in all fairness to the occu-
pants, it can be pointed out that after twilight, when
shadows and weak bulbs work their magic, the room
becomes interesting.

On a table near the front left of the room is a small wire cage designed to hold a rabbit. Near this are several school books, notebook papers, and other weapons of high school children. A kitchen area, boasting a hot plate, has been carved near the bottom of the staircase, and the window, which was formerly the front of the vegetable store, is now mostly covered with old newspapers so that passersby cannot see in. A bit of the clear glass remains at the top—but drab, lifeless drapes line the sides of the window.

ACT I

The lights go down slowly as music creeps in—
a theme for lost children, the near misbegotten.
From the blackness TILLIE'S VOICE *speaks against*
the music.

TILLIE'S VOICE:

He told me to look at my hand, for a part of it
came from a star that exploded too long ago to
imagine. This part of me was formed from a
tongue of fire that screamed through the heav-
ens until there was our sun. And this part of
me—this tiny part of me—was on the sun
when it itself exploded and whirled in a great
storm until the planets came to be.

Lights start in.

And this small part of me was then a whisper
of the earth. When there was life, perhaps this
part of me got lost in a fern that was crushed
and covered until it was coal. And then it was
a diamond millions of years later—it must
have been a diamond as beautiful as the star
from which it had first come.

TILLIE: *Taking over from recorded voice.*

Or perhaps this part of me became lost in a
terrible beast, or became part of a huge bird

that flew above the primeval swamps.

And he said this thing was so small—this part of me was so small it couldn't be seen—but it was there from the beginning of the world.

And he called this bit of me an atom. And when he wrote the word, I fell in love with it.

Atom.

Atom.

What a beautiful word.

The phone rings.

BEATRICE: *Off stage.*
Will you get that please?

The phone rings again before BEATRICE *appears in her bathrobe from the kitchen.*

No help! Never any help!

She answers the phone.

Hello? Yes it is. Who is this? . . . I hope there

hasn't been any trouble at school . . . Oh, she's always been like that. She hardly says a word around here, either. I always say some people were born to speak and others born to listen . . .

You know I've been meaning to call you to thank you for that lovely rabbit you gave Matilda. She and I just adore it and it's gotten so big . . .

Well, it certainly was thoughtful. Mr. Goodman, I don't mean to change the subject but aren't you that delightful young man Tillie said hello to a couple of months back at the A & P? You were by the lobster tank and I was near the frozen foods? That delightful and handsome young man? . . . Why, I would very much indeed use the expression *handsome*. Yes, and . . .

Well, I encourage her at every opportunity at home. Did she say I didn't? Both my daughters have their own desks and I put 75-watt bulbs right near them . . . Yes . . . Yes . . . I think those tests are very much overrated, anyway, Mr. Goodman . . . Well, believe me she's nothing like that around this house . . .

Now I don't want you to think I don't appreciate what you're trying to do, Mr. Goodman, but I'm afraid it's simply useless. I've tried just everything, but she isn't a pretty girl—I mean, let's be frank about it—she's going to have her problems. Are you married, Mr. Goodman?

Oh, that's too bad. I don't know what's the matter with women today letting a handsome young man like you get away . . .

Well, some days she just doesn't feel like going to school. You just said how bright she is, and I'm really afraid to put too much of a strain on her after what happened to her sister. You know, too much strain is the worst thing in this modern world, Mr. Goodman, and I can't afford to have another convulsive on my hands, now can I? But don't you worry about Matilda. There will be some place for her in this world. And, like I said, some were born to speak and others just to listen . . . and do call again, Mr. Goodman. It's been a true pleasure speaking with you. Goodbye.

BEATRICE *hangs up the phone and advances into the main room. The lights come up.*

Matilda, that wasn't very nice of you to tell them I was forcibly detaining you from school. Why, the way that Mr. Goodman spoke, he must think I'm running a concentration camp. Do you have any idea how embarrassing it is to be accused of running a concentration camp for your own children?

Well, it isn't embarrassing at all.

That school of yours is forty years behind the times anyway, and believe me you learn more around here than that ugly Mr. Goodman can teach you!

You know, I really feel sorry for him. I never saw a man with a more effeminate face in my life. When I saw you talking to him by the lobster tank I said to myself, "Good Lord, for a science teacher my poor girl has got herself a Hebrew hermaphrodite." Of course, he's not as bad as Miss Hanley. The idea of letting her teach girl's gym is staggering.

And you have to place me in the embarrassing position of giving them a reason to call me at eight-thirty in the morning, no less.

TILLIE:
    I didn't say anything.

BEATRICE:
    What do you tell them when they want to
    know why you stay home once in a while?

TILLIE:
    I tell them I'm sick.

BEATRICE:
    Oh, you're sick all right, the exact nature of
    the illness not fully realized, but you're sick all
    right. Any daughter that would turn her
    mother in as the administrator of a concentra-
    tion camp has got to be suffering from some-
    thing very peculiar.

TILLIE:
    Can I go in today, Mother?

BEATRICE:
    You'll go in, all right.

TILLIE:
    Mr. Goodman said he was going to do an
    experiment—

BEATRICE:

Why, he looks like the kind that would do his experimenting after sundown.

TILLIE:

On radioactivity—

BEATRICE:

On radioactivity? That's all that high school needs!

TILLIE:

He's going to bring in the cloud chamber—

BEATRICE:

Why, what an outstanding event. If you had warned me yesterday I would've gotten all dressed to kill and gone with you today. I love seeing cloud chambers being brought in.

TILLIE:

You can actually see—

BEATRICE:

You're giving me a headache.

TILLIE:

Please?

BEATRICE:

No, my dear, the fortress of knowledge is not going to be blessed with your presence today. I have a good number of exciting duties for you to take care of, not the least of which is rabbit droppings.

TILLIE:

Oh, Mother, please . . . I'll do it after school.

BEATRICE:

If we wait a minute longer this house is going to ferment. I found rabbit droppings in my bedroom even.

TILLIE:

I could do it after Mr. Goodman's class. I'll say I'm ill and ask for a sick pass.

BEATRICE:

Do you want me to chloroform that thing right this minute?

TILLIE:

No!

BEATRICE:

Then shut up.

RUTH *comes to the top of the stairs. She is dressed for school, and though her clothes are simple she gives the impression of being slightly strange. Her hair isn't quite combed, her sweater doesn't quite fit, etc.*

RUTH:
Do you have Devil's Kiss down there?

BEATRICE:
It's in the bathroom cabinet.

RUTH *comes downstairs and goes to the bathroom door, located under the stairs. She flings it open and rummages in the cabinet.*

RUTH:
There's so much junk in here it's driving me crazy.

BEATRICE:
Maybe it's in my purse . . . If you don't hurry up you'll be late for school.

RUTH:
Well, I couldn't very well go in without Devil's Kiss, now could I?

BEATRICE:

> Doesn't anyone go to school these days with-
> out that all over their lips?

RUTH: *Finding the lipstick.*

> Nobody I know, except Tillie, that is. And if she
> had a little lipstick on I'll bet they wouldn't
> have laughed at her so much yesterday.

BEATRICE:

> Why were they laughing?

RUTH:

> The assembly. Didn't she tell you about the
> assembly?

BEATRICE:

> Ruth, you didn't tell me she was in an assembly.

RUTH:

> Well, I just thought of it right now. How could
> I tell you anything until I think of it—did you
> ever stop to consider that? Some crummy sci-
> ence assembly.

BEATRICE: *To* TILLIE.

> What is she talking about?

RUTH:

> I thought she'd tell the whole world. Imagine,
> right in front of the assembly, with everybody
> laughing at her.

BEATRICE:

> Will you be quiet, Ruth? *Why were they laugh-
> ing at you?*

TILLIE:

> I don't know.

RUTH:

> You don't know? My heavens, she was a sight.
> She had that old jumper on—the faded one
> with the low collar—and a raggy slip that
> showed all over and her hair looked like she
> was struck by lightning.

BEATRICE:

> You're exaggerating . . .

RUTH:

> She was cranking this model of something—

TILLIE:

> The atom.

RUTH:

This model of the atom . . . you know, it had this crank and a long tower so that when you turned it these little colored balls went spinning around like crazy. And there was Tillie, cranking away, looking weird as a coot . . . that old jumper with the raggy slip and the lightning hair . . . cranking away while some boy with glasses was reading this stupid speech . . . and everybody burst into laughter until the teachers yelled at them. And all day long, the kids kept coming up to me saying, "Is that really your sister? How can you bear it?" And you know, Chris Burns says to me— "*She* looks like the one that went to the looney doctors." I could have kissed him there and then.

BEATRICE: *Taking a backscratcher*.

Matilda, if you can't get yourself dressed properly before going to school you're never going to go again. I don't like the idea of everybody laughing at you, because when they laugh at you they're laughing at me. And I don't want you cranking any more . . . atoms.

RUTH: *Putting the lipstick back in* BEATRICE's *bag*.

You're almost out of Devil's Kiss.

BEATRICE:
> If you didn't put so much on it would last longer.

RUTH:
> Who was that calling?

BEATRICE:
> Matilda turned me in to the Gestapo.

RUTH:
> Can I earn a cigarette this morning?

BEATRICE:
> Why not?

> BEATRICE *offers her the backscratcher along with a cigarette.*

RUTH:
> Was it Mr. Goodman?

BEATRICE:
> Who?

RUTH: *Lighting the cigarette.*
> The call this morning. Was it Mr. Goodman?

BEATRICE:
> Yes.

RUTH: *Using the backscratcher on* BEATRICE, *who squirms with ecstasy.*
>I figured it would be.

BEATRICE:
>A little higher, please.

RUTH:
>There?

BEATRICE:
>Yes, *there* . . . Why did you figure it would be Mr. Goodman?

RUTH:
>Well, he called me out of sewing class yesterday—I remember because my blouse wasn't all buttoned—and he wanted to know why Tillie's out of school so much.

BEATRICE:
>Lower. A little lower . . . And what did you tell him?

RUTH:
>I wish you'd go back to Kools. I liked Kools better.

TILLIE: *Gravely concerned.*
    What did you tell him?

RUTH:
    I told him you were ill, and he wanted to know what kind, so I told him you had leprosy.

TILLIE:
    You didn't!

RUTH:
    You should have seen his face. He was so cute. And I told him you had ringworm and gangrene.

BEATRICE:
    What did he say?

RUTH:
    And I told him you had what Mother's last patient had . . . whatchamacallit?

BEATRICE:
    Psoriasis?

RUTH:
    Yeah. Something like that.

TILLIE:

Tell me you didn't, Ruth!

RUTH:

O.K. I didn't . . . But I really did.

BEATRICE:

He knew you were joking.

RUTH:

And then I told him to go look up the *history* and then he'd find out. Whenever they go look up the history then they don't bother me any-more 'cause they think I'm crazy.

BEATRICE:

Ruth—

RUTH:

And I told him the disease you had was fatal and that there wasn't much hope for you.

BEATRICE:

What kind of *history* is it?

RUTH:

Just a little folder with the story of our lives in it, that's all.

BEATRICE:

How did you ever see it?

RUTH:

I read the whole thing last term when Miss Hanley dragged me into the record room because I didn't want to climb the ropes in gym and I told her my skull was growing.

BEATRICE:

A little *lower*, please.

RUTH:

Lower! Higher! I wish you'd make up your mind. If you'd switch back to Kools it might be worth it, but ugh! these are awful. You know, I really did think my skull was growing. Either that or a tumor. So she dragged me out of gym class, and she thought I couldn't read upside down while she was sitting opposite me with the history. But I could.

BEATRICE:

What does it say?

RUTH:

Oh, it says you're divorced and that I went crazy . . . and my father took a heart attack at Star Lake . . . and now you're a widow—

BEATRICE: *Referring to the backscratching.*
That's it! Hold it right there! Aaah!

RUTH:
And it says that I exaggerate and tell stories
and that I'm afraid of death and have nightmares . . . and all that stuff.

BEATRICE:
And what else does it say?

RUTH:
I can't remember everything you know.
Remember this, remember that . . . remember
this, that . . .

Go to dark. Music in.

TILLIE'S VOICE:
Today I saw it. Behind the glass a white cloud
began to form. He placed a small piece of metal
in the center of the chamber and we waited
until I saw the first one—a trace of smoke that
came from nowhere and then disappeared.
And then another . . . and another, until I knew
it was coming from the metal. They looked
like water-sprays from a park fountain, and
they went on and on for as long as I watched.

And he told me the fountain of smoke would come forth for a long time, and if I had wanted to, I could have stayed there all my life and it would never have ended—that fountain, so close I could have touched it. In front of my eyes, one part of the world was becoming another. Atoms exploding, flinging off tiny bullets that caused the fountain, atom after atom breaking down into something new. And no one could stop the fountain. It would go on for millions of years—on and on, this fountain from eternity.

By the end of this speech, the lights are on to show TILLIE *preparing boxes of dirt in which to plant seeds. The rabbit is in the cage near her, and* BEATRICE *is reading a newspaper on the other side of the room. She is sipping coffee from a huge coffee cup.*

BEATRICE:
I thought we had everything, but leave it to you to think of the one thing we're missing . . .

She reads from the newspaper.

Twenty-two acres in Prince's Bay. Small pond. $6,000 . . . That's cheap. I'd take a look at it if I had any money . . .

What kind of seeds are they?

TILLIE:

Marigolds. They've been exposed to cobalt-60.

BEATRICE:

If there's one thing I've always wanted, it's been a living room planted with marigolds that have been exposed to cobalt-60. While you're at it, why don't you throw in a tomato patch in the bathroom?

TILLIE:

Just let me keep them here for a week or so until they get started and then I'll transplant them to the backyard.

BEATRICE: *Reading again.*

Four-family house. Six and a half and six and a half over five and five. Eight garages. I could really do something with that. A nursing home . . .

Don't think I'm not kicking myself that I didn't finish that real estate course. I should have finished beauty school, too . . .

God, what I could do with eight garages . . .

There is a sound from beyond the curtained doorway. BEATRICE *gestures in that direction.*

You know, I'm thinking of getting rid of *that* and making this place into something.

TILLIE:
Yes.

BEATRICE:
I've been thinking about a tea shop.

Have you noticed there aren't many of them around anymore?

TILLIE:
Yes.

BEATRICE:
And this is just the type of neighborhood where a good tea shop could make a go of it. We'd have a good cheesecake. You've got to have a good cheesecake . . .

She calculates.

Eight times ten—well, eight times eight, if they're falling down—that's sixty-four dollars a month from the garages alone . . . I swear money makes money.

There is a rustling at the curtains. Two thin and wrinkled hands push the curtains apart slowly and then the ancient face of NANNY *appears. She negotiates her way through the curtains. She is utterly wrinkled and dried, perhaps a century old. Time has left her with a whisper of a smile—a smile from a soul half-departed. If one looked closely, great cataracts could be seen on each eye, and it is certain that all that can pierce her soundless prison are mere shadows from the outside world. She pervades the room with age.*

NANNY *supports herself by a four-legged tubular frame which she pushes along in front of her with a shuffling motion that reminds one of a ticking clock. Inch by inch she advances into the room.* TILLIE *and* BEATRICE *continue speaking, knowing that it will be minutes before she is close enough to know they are there.*

BEATRICE:
What is cobalt-60?

TILLIE:
It's something that causes . . . changes in seeds.

Oh, Mother—he set the cloud chamber up just for me and he told me about radioactivity and half-life and he got the seeds for me.

BEATRICE: *Her attention still on the newspaper.*
What does half-life mean?

NANNY *is well into the room as* TILLIE *replies.*

TILLIE: *Reciting from memory.*
The half-life of Polonium-210 is one hundred and forty days.

The half-life of Radium-226 is one thousand five hundred and ninety years.

The half-life of Uranium-238 is four and one-half billion years.

BEATRICE: *Putting away her newspaper.*
Do you know you're giving me a headache?

Then, in a loud, horribly saccharine voice, she speaks to NANNY *as if she were addressing a deaf year-old child.*

LOOK WHO'S THERE! IT'S NANNY!

NANNY CAME ALL THE WAY OUT
HERE BY HERSELF!

I'm going to need a cigarette for this.

NANNY! YOU COME SIT DOWN AND
WE'LL BE RIGHT WITH HER!

You know, sometimes I've got to laugh. I've
got *this* on my hands and all you're worried
about is planting marigolds.

I'VE GOT HOTSY WATER FOR YOU,
NANNY. WOULD YOU LIKE SOME
HOTSY WATER AND HONEY?

NANNY *has seated herself at a table, smiling but
oblivious to her environment.*

I've never seen it to fail. Every time I decide to
have a cup of coffee I see that face at the curtains. I wonder what she'd do . . .

She holds a pot of boiling water.

. . . if I just poured this right over her head. I'll
bet she wouldn't even notice it.

NANNY'S GOING TO GET JUST WHAT SHE NEEDS!

She fills a cup for her and places a honey jar near her.

You know if someone told me when I was young that I'd end up feeding honey to a zombie, I'd tell them they were crazy.

SOMETHING WRONG, NANNY? OH, DID I FORGET NANNY'S SPOON? MERCY! MERCY! I FORGOT NANNY'S SPOON!

She gets a spoon and stands behind NANNY.

I'll give you a spoon, Nanny, I'll give you a spoon.

She makes a motion behind NANNY'S *back as if she's going to smack her on the head with the spoon.*

Matilda! Watch me give Nanny her spoon.

A SPOON FOR NANNY!

It manages to be slightly funny and TILLIE *yields to a laugh, along with her mother.*

Fifty dollars a week. Fifty dollars. I look at you, Nanny, and I wonder if it's worth it. I think I'd be better off driving a cab.

TAKE HONEY, NANNY. HONEY WITH HOTSY WATER!

You should have seen her daughter bring her here last week . . . I could have used you that day . . . She came in pretending she was Miss Career Woman of the Year. She said she was in real estate and *such a busy little woman*, such a busy little woman—she just couldn't give all the love and care and affection her little momsy needed anymore . . .

Then, with a great smile, she speaks right into NANNY *'s uncomprehending face.*

Nanny's quite a little cross to bear, now aren't you, Nanny dear? But you're a little better than Mr. Mayo was—with the tumor on his brain—or Miss Marion Minto with her cancer, or Mr. Brougham . . . what was his first name?

TILLIE:
Alexander.

BEATRICE:

> Mr. Alexander Brougham with the worms in his legs.

> WHY, NANNY'S QUITE SOME LITTLE GIRL, AREN'T YOU, NANNY? A GIRL DRINKING HER HOTSY AND HONEY! . . . Cobalt-60. Ha! You take me for a fool, don't you?

TILLIE:

> No, Mother.

BEATRICE:

> Science, science, science! Don't they teach our misfits anything anymore? Anything decent and meaningful and sensitive? Do you know what I'd be now if it wasn't for this mud pool I got sucked into? I'd probably be a dancer. Miss Betty Frank, The Best Dancer of the Class of 19 . . . something. One minute I'm the best dancer in school—smart as a whip—the head of the whole crowd! And the next minute . . .

> One mistake. That's how it starts. Marry the wrong man and before you know it he's got you tied down with two stones around your neck for the rest of your life.

When I was in that lousy high school I was one of the most respected kids you ever saw.

I used to wonder why people always said, "Why, just yesterday . . . why, just yesterday . . . why, just yesterday . . ."

Before I knew what happened I lost my dancing legs and got varicose legs. Beautiful varicose legs. Do you know, everything I ever thought I'd be has exploded!

NANNY, YOU HURRY UP WITH THAT HONEY!

Exploded! You know, I almost forgot about everything I was supposed to be . . .

NANNY'S ALMOST FINISHED. ISN'T THAT WONDERFUL?

She's almost finished, all right.

NANNY'S DAUGHTER IS COMING TO SEE YOU SOON. WILL THAT MAKE NANNY HAPPY?

The day Miss Career Woman of the Year

comes to visit again I think I'll drop dead. Nobody's too busy for anything they want to do, don't you tell me. What kind of an idiot do people take me for?

NANNY, YOU'RE SPILLING YOUR HOTSY! JESUS CHRIST!

You know, I ought to kick you right out and open that tea shop tomorrow.

Oh, it's coming. I can feel it. And the first thing I'll do is get rid of that rabbit.

TILLIE: *Hardly listening.*
Yes, Mother.

BEATRICE:
You think I'm kidding?

TILLIE:
No, I don't.

BEATRICE:
You bet I'm not!

She rummages through some drawers in a chest.

I was going to do this a month ago.

She holds up a small bottle.

Here it is. Here's a new word for you.

She reads.

Trichloro . . . methane. Do you know what that is, Matilda? Well, it's chloroform!

She puts the bottle away.

I'm saving it for that Angora manure machine of yours. Speaking of manure machines, IS NANNY READY TO GO MAKE DUTY?

She starts helping NANNY *out of the chair and props her up with the tubular frame.*

NANNY IS ALWAYS READY FOR DUTY, AREN'T YOU NANNY? BECAUSE NANNY'S A GOODY-GOODY GIRL AND GOODY-GOODY GIRLS ALWAYS GET GOODY-GOODY THINGS. GOD LOOKS OUT FOR GOODY-GOODY GIRLS AND GIVES THEM HOTSY AND HONEY—RIGHT, NANNY?

BEATRICE *sits down in the hall and watches* NANNY *make her way toward the bathroom. There is a pause as the woman's shuffling continues.*

The lights go low on TILLIE, NANNY *becomes a silhouette, and the light remains on* BEATRICE. *She starts to read the paper again, but the shuffling gets on her nerves and she flings the paper down.*

Half-life! If you want to know what a half-life is, just ask me. You're looking at the original half-life!

I got stuck with one daughter with half a mind; another one who's half a test tube; half a husband—a house half full of rabbit crap—and half a corpse!

That's what I call a half-life, Matilda! Me and cobalt-60! Two of the biggest half-*lifes* you ever saw!

The set goes to dark.

After a few seconds, the sound of someone dialing a phone can be heard. As the spot comes up on her, we see BEATRICE *holding the phone and struggling to get a cigarette.*

BEATRICE: *On the phone.*
Hello—Mr. Goodman, please . . . How would

I know if he's got a class? . . . Hello, Mr. Goodman? Are you Mr. Goodman? . . . Oh, I beg your pardon, Miss Torgersen . . . Yes, I'll wait . . .

She lights her cigarette.

Couldn't you find him, Miss Torgersen? . . . Oh! Excuse me, Mr. Goodman. How are you? . . . I'll bet you'll never guess who this is—it's Mrs. Hunsdorfer—remember the frozen foods?

She laughs.

You know, Ruth told me she's your new secretary and I certainly think that's a delight. You were paying so much attention to Matilda that I'll bet Ruth just got jealous. She does things like that, you know. I hope she works hard for you, although I can't imagine what kind of work Ruth could be doing in that great big science office. She's a terrible snoop . . .

She takes a puff.

Your attendance? Isn't that charming. And the *cut* cards! Imagine. You trust her with . . . why, I didn't know she could type *at all* . . . imagine.

Well . . . I'll . . . Of course, *too* much work isn't good for anyone, either. No wonder she's failing everything. I mean, I never knew a girl who failed everything regardless of what they were suffering from. I suppose I should say *recovering* from . . .

Well, it's about the seeds you gave Matilda . . . Well, she's had them in the house for a week now and they're starting to grow. Now, she told me they had been subjected to radioactivity, and I hear such terrible things about radioactivity that I automatically associate radioactivity with sterility, and it positively horrifies me to have those seeds right here in my living room. Couldn't she just grow plain marigolds like everyone else?

She takes a puff.

Oh . . .

Another big puff, forming a mushroom cloud.

It does sound like an interesting project, but . . .

The biggest puff yet.

No, I must admit that at this very moment I don't know what a *mutation* is . . .

She laughs uncomfortably.

Mr. Goodman . . . Mr. Goodman! I don't want you to think I'm not interested, but please spare me definitions over the phone. I'll go to the library next week and pick me out some little book on science and then I'll know all about mutations . . . No, you didn't insult me, but I just want you to know that I'm not *stupid* . . .

I just thought prevention was better than a tragedy, Mr. Goodman. I mean, Matilda has enough problems to worry about without *sterility* . . .

Well, I was just concerned, but you've put my poor mother's heart at ease. You know, really, our schools need more exciting young men like you, I really mean that. Really. Oh, I do. Goodbye, Mr. Goodman.

By the end of her talk on the phone, her face is left in a spotlight, and then the stage goes black. The music theme comes in, in a minor key, softly at first, but accentuated by increasingly loud pulses which transmute into thunder crashes.

There is a scream heard from upstairs and we see the set in night shadows.

TILLIE *tears open her bedroom door and rushes into* BEATRICE's *room.* RUTH *screams again.*

TILLIE:
Mother! She's going to have one!

RUTH *appears on the landing and releases another scream which breaks off into gasps. She starts down the stairs and stops halfway to scream again. There is another tremendous thunder crash as* BEATRICE *comes out of her room, puts on the hall light, and catches the hysterical girl on the stairs.*

BEATRICE: *Shouting.*
Stop it! Stop it, Ruth!

TILLIE: *At the top of the stairs.*
She's going!

BEATRICE:
Ruth! Stop it!

TILLIE:
> She's going to go!

BEATRICE: *Yelling at* TILLIE.
> Shut up and get back in your room!

> RUTH *screams.*

> You're not going to let yourself go, do you
> hear me, Ruth? You're not going to go!

RUTH:
> He's after me!

> *She screams, lightning and thunder crash follow.*

BEATRICE:
> You were dreaming, do you hear me?
> Nobody's after you! Nobody!

TILLIE:
> I saw her eyes start to go back—

BEATRICE: *To* TILLIE.
> Get back in your room!

> *She helps* RUTH *down the rest of the stairs*

There, now, nobody's after you. Nice and easy. Breathe deeply . . . Did the big bad man come after my little girl?

She sits RUTH *down and then puts both hands up to her own face and pulls her features into a comic mask.* RUTH *begins to laugh at her.*

That big bad bogey man?

They both laugh heartily.

Now that wasn't so bad, was it?

RUTH:
It was the dream, with Mr. Mayo again.

BEATRICE:
Oh. Well, we'll just get you a little hot milk and—

A tremendous thunder crash throws the set into shadows.

Why, the electricity's gone off. Do you remember what happened to those candles?

RUTH:
What candles?

BEATRICE:
>The little white ones from my birthday cake last year.

RUTH:
>Tillie melted them down for school a long time ago.

BEATRICE: *Searching through drawers*.
>She had no right doing that.

RUTH:
>She asked you. She used them to attach a paper straw to a milk bottle with a balloon over it, and it was supposed to tell if it was going to rain.

BEATRICE: *Finding a flashlight*.
>There! It works. I don't want her wasting anything of mine unless she's positive I won't need it. You always need candles.

She steers RUTH *toward the couch as lightning flashes*.

>Why, Ruth—your skin just turned ice cold!

She rummages through one of the boxes and grabs a blanket.

This will warm you up . . . What's the matter?

RUTH:
The flashlight—

BEATRICE:
What's wrong with it?

RUTH:
It's the same one I used to check on Mr. Mayo with.

BEATRICE:
So it is. We don't need it.

RUTH:
No, let me keep it.

Starting to laugh.

Do you want to know how they have it in the history?

BEATRICE:
No, I don't.

RUTH:
Well, they say I came out of my room . . .

She flashes the light on her room.

. . . And I started down the stairs, step by step . . . and I heard the choking and banging on the bed, and . . .

BEATRICE:
I'm going back to bed.

RUTH:
No!

BEATRICE:
Well, talk about something nice, then.

RUTH:
Oh, Mama, tell me about the wagon.

BEATRICE:
You change so fast I can't keep up with you.

RUTH:
Mama, *please* . . . the story about the wagon.

BEATRICE:
I don't know anything about telling stories. Get those great big smart teachers of yours to do that sort of stuff.

RUTH:

Tell me about the horses again, and how you stole the wagon.

BEATRICE:

Don't get me started on that.

RUTH:

Mama, *please* . . .

BEATRICE: *Taking out a pack of cigarettes.*

Do you want a cigarette?

RUTH: *Taking one.*

Leave out the part where they shoot the horses, though.

They both light up.

BEATRICE:

Honey, you know the whole story—

RUTH:

"Apples! Pears! *Cu* . . . cumbers!"

BEATRICE:

No. It's "Apples! Pears! *Cucum* . . . bers!"

They say it together.

"Apples! Pears! *Cucum* . . . bers!"

And they laugh.

RUTH:
How did you get the wagon out without him seeing you?

BEATRICE:
That was easy. Every time he got home for the day he'd make us both some sandwiches—my mama had been dead for years—and he'd take a nap on the old sofa that used to be . . . there!

She points to a corner of the room.

And while he was sleeping I got the horses hitched up and went riding around the block waving to everyone.

RUTH:
Oh, Mama, you didn't!

BEATRICE:
Of course I did. I had more nerve than a bear

when I was a kid. Let me tell you it takes nerve to sit up on that wagon every day yelling "Apples! . . ."

Both together.

"Pears! *Cucum* . . . bers!"

They laugh again.

RUTH:
Did he find out you took the wagon?

BEATRICE:
Did he find out? He came running down the street after me and started spanking me right on top of the wagon—not hard—but it was so embarrassing—and I had one of those penny marshmallow ships in the back pocket of my overalls, and it got all squished. And you better believe I never did it again . . .

You would have loved him, Ruth, and gone out with him on the wagon . . . all over Stapleton yelling as loud as you wanted.

RUTH:
"Apples! Pears! *Cu* . . . cumbers!"

BEATRICE:
    No!

RUTH:
    "*Cucum* . . . bers!"

BEATRICE:
    My father made up for all the other men in this
    whole world, Ruth. If only you two could have
    met. He'd only be about seventy now, do you
    realize that? And I'll bet he'd still be selling
    vegetables around town. All that fun—and then
    I don't think I ever knew what really hit me.

RUTH:
    Don't tell about—

BEATRICE:
    Don't worry about the horses.

RUTH:
    What hit you?

BEATRICE:
    Well it was just me and Papa . . . and your
    father hanging around. And then Papa got
    sick . . . and I drove with him up to the sana-
    torium. And then I came home and there

were the horses—

RUTH:
   Mother!

BEATRICE:
   And I had the horses . . . taken care of. And
   then Papa got terribly sick and he begged me to
   marry so that he'd be sure I'd be taken care of.

   She laughs.

   If he knew how I was taken care of he'd turn
   over in his grave.

   And *nightmares*! Do you want to know the
   nightmare I used to have?

   I never had nightmares over the fights with
   your father, or the divorce, or his thrombo-
   sis—he deserved it—I never had nightmares
   over any of that.

   Let me tell you about my nightmare that used
   to come back and back:

   Well, I'm on Papa's wagon, but it's newer and

shinier, and it's being pulled by beautiful white horses, not dirty workhorses—these are like circus horses with long manes and tinsel—and the wagon is blue, shiny blue. And it's full—filled with yellow apples and grapes and green squash.

You're going to laugh when you hear this. I'm wearing a lovely gown with jewels all over it, and my hair is piled up on top of my head with a long feather in it, and the bells are ringing.

Huge bells swinging on a gold braid strung across the back of the wagon, and they're going DONG, DONG . . . DONG, DONG. And I'm yelling "APPLES! PEARS! CUCUM . . . BERS!"

RUTH:

That doesn't sound like a nightmare to me.

BEATRICE:

And then I turn down our street and all the noise stops. This long street, with all the doors of the houses shut and everything crowded next to each other, and there's not a soul around. And then I start getting afraid that the vegetables are going to spoil . . . and that nobody's going to buy anything, and I feel as though I shouldn't be on the wagon, and I keep trying to call out.

But there isn't a sound. Not a single sound. Then I turn my head and look at the house across the street. I see an upstairs window, and a pair of hands pull the curtains slowly apart. I see the face of my father and my heart stands still . . .

Ruth . . . take the light out of my eyes.

A long pause.

RUTH:
Is Nanny going to die here?

BEATRICE:
No.

RUTH:
How can you be sure?

BEATRICE:
I can tell.

RUTH:
    Are you crying?

BEATRICE:
    What's left for me, Ruth?

RUTH:
    What, Mama?

BEATRICE:
    What's left for me?

*The stage goes slowly to dark as the drizzling rain
becomes louder and then disappears.*

When the lights come up again NANNY *is seated at
the kitchen table with a bottle of beer and a glass in
front of her.* TILLIE *comes in the front door with a
box of large marigold plants and sets them down
where they'll be inconspicuous. She gets the rabbit
out of its cage, sits down near* NANNY *and gives her
a little wave.* BEATRICE *suddenly appears at the top
of the stairs and drops a stack of newspapers with a
loud thud. She goes back into her room and lets fly
another armful of junk.*

TILLIE:

What are you doing?

BEATRICE:

A little housecleaning, and you're going to help. You can start by getting rid of that rabbit or I'll suffocate the bastard.

She takes a drink from a glass of whiskey.

You don't think I will, do you? You wait and see. Where's Ruth? She's probably running around the school-yard in her brassiere.

She comes downstairs.

TILLIE:

Mother, they want me to do something at school.

BEATRICE:

NANNY! DID YOU HEAR THAT? THEY WANT HER TO DO SOMETHING AT SCHOOL! ISN'T THAT MOMENTOUS, NANNY?

Well I want you to do something around here. Like get rid of that bunny. I'm being generous! I'll let you give it away. Far away. Give it to Mr.

Goodman. I'd chloroform the thing myself, but that crazy sister of yours would throw convulsions for fifty years . . . and I hate a house that vibrates.

And get rid of those sterile marigolds. They stink!

HI, NANNY—HOW ARE YOU, HONEY? HOW WOULD YOU LIKE TO GO ON A LONG TRIP?

You see, everybody, I spent today taking stock of my life and I've come up with zero. I added up all the separate departments and the total reads zero . . .

zero zero zero zero zero zero zero zero zero zero zero zero

zero zero zero
zero zero
zero

. . . And do you know how you pronounce that, with all your grammatical schoolin' and foolin'? You pronounce it o, o, o, o, O, O, O, O, O, O! o, o, o, o, O, O, O, O, O, O, O, O!

Right, Nanny? RIGHT, NANNY?

So, by the end of the week, you get rid of that cottontail compost heap and we'll get you a job down at the five-and-ten-cent store. And if you don't do so well with the public, we'll fix you up with some kind of machine. Wouldn't that be nice?

RUTH *enters at a gallop, throwing her books down and babbling a mile a minute.*

RUTH: *Enthusiastically.*
Can you believe it? I didn't, until Chris Burns came up and told me about it in Geography, and then Mr. Goodman told me himself during the eighth period in the office when I was eavesdropping. Aren't you so happy you could bust? Tillie? I'm so proud I can't believe it, Mama. Everybody was talking about it and nobody . . . well, it was the first time they all came up screaming about her and I said, "Yes, she's my sister!" I said it, "She's my sister! My sister! My *sister*!" Give me a cigarette.

BEATRICE:
Get your hands off my personal property.

RUTH:

I'll scratch your back later.

BEATRICE:

I don't want you to touch me!

RUTH:

Did he call yet? My God, I can't believe it, I just can't!

BEATRICE:

Did who call yet?

RUTH:

I'm not supposed to tell you, as Mr. Goodman's private secretary, but you're going to get a call from school.

BEATRICE: *To* TILLIE.

What is she talking about?

TILLIE:

I was in the Science Fair at school.

RUTH:

Didn't she tell you yet? Oh, Tillie, how could you? She's fantastic, Mama! She's a finalist in the Science Fair. There were only five of them out of hundreds and hundreds. She won with all those plants over there. They're freaks! Isn't that a scream? Dr. Berg picked her himself. The principal! And I heard Mr. Goodman say she was going to be another Madam Pasteur and he never saw a girl do anything like that before and . . . so I told everybody, "Yes, she's my sister!" Tillie, "You're my sister!" I said. And Mr. Goodman called the Advance and they're coming to take your picture. Oh, Mama, isn't it crazy? And nobody laughed at her, Mama. She beat out practically everybody and nobody laughed at her. "She's my sister," I said. "She's my sister!"

The telephone rings.

That must be him! Mama, answer it—I'm afraid.

Ring.

Answer it before he hangs up!

Ring.

Mama! He's gonna hang up!

RUTH *grabs the phone.*

Hello? . . . Yes . . .

Aside to BEATRICE.

It's him! . . . Just a minute, please . . .

Covering the mouthpiece.

He wants to talk to you.

BEATRICE:
Who?

RUTH:
The *principal*!

BEATRICE:
Hang up.

RUTH:
I told him you were here! Mama!

BEATRICE *gets up and shuffles slowly to the phone.*

BEATRICE: *Finally, into the phone.*
Yes? . . . I know who you are, Dr. Berg . . . I
see . . . Couldn't you get someone else? There's
an awful lot of work that has to be done
around here, because she's not as careful with
her home duties as she is with man-in-the-
moon marigolds . . .

Me? What would you want with me up on the stage? . . . The other mothers can do as they please . . . I would have thought you had enough in your *history* without . . . I'll think about it . . . Goodbye, Dr. Berg . . .

Pause, then screaming.

I SAID I'D THINK ABOUT IT!

She hangs up the phone, turns her face slowly to RUTH, *then to* TILLIE, *who has her face hidden in shame in the rabbit's fur.*

RUTH:
What did he say?

BEATRICE: *Flinging her glass on the floor.*

How could you do this to me? HOW COULD YOU LET THAT MAN CALL OUR HOME!

I have no clothes, do you hear me? I'd look just like you up on the stage, ugly little you!

DO YOU WANT THEM TO LAUGH AT US? LAUGH AT THE TWO OF US?

RUTH: *Disbelievingly.*
>
> Mother . . . aren't you proud of her?
>
> Mother . . . it's an *honor*.

TILLIE *breaks into tears and moves away from* BEATRICE. *It seems as though she is crushed, but then she halts and turns to face her mother.*

TILLIE: *Through tears.*
>
> But . . . nobody laughed at me.

BEATRICE'*s face begins to soften as she glimpses what she's done to* TILLIE.

BEATRICE:
>
> Oh, my God . . .

TILLIE *starts toward her.* BEATRICE *opens her arms to receive her as music starts in and lights fade. A chord of finality punctuates the end of Act I.*

ACT II

About two weeks later.

The room looks somewhat cheery and there is excitement in the air. It is early evening and preparations are being made for TILLIE *to take her project to the final judging of the Science Fair.*

TILLIE *has been dressed by her mother in clothes which are clean but too girlish for her awkwardness. Her hair has been curled, she sports a large bow, and her dress is a starched flair.*

RUTH *has dressed herself up as well. She has put on too much makeup, and her lipstick has been extended beyond the natural line of her lips. She almost appears to be sinister.*

A large three-panel screen stands on one of the tables. THE EFFECT OF GAMMA RAYS ON MAN-IN-THE-MOON MARIGOLDS is printed in large letters running across the top of the three panels. Below this on each panel there is a subtopic: THE PAST; THE PRESENT; THE FUTURE. *Additional charts and data appear below the titles.*

RUTH:

The only competition you have to worry about is Janice Vickery. They say she caught it near

Princess Bay Boulevard and it was still alive when she took the skin off it.

TILLIE: *Taking some plants from* RUTH.
Let me do that, please, Ruth.

RUTH:
I'm sorry I touched them, really.

TILLIE:
Why don't you feed Peter?

RUTH:
Because I don't feel like feeding him . . . Now I feel like feeding him.

She gets some lettuce from a bag.

I heard that it screamed for three minutes after she put it in because the water wasn't boiling yet. How much talent does it take to boil the skin off a cat and then stick the bones together again? That's what I want to know. Ugh. I had a dream about that, too. I figure she did it in less than a day and she ends up as one of the top five winners . . . and you spend months growing atomic flowers.

TILLIE:

Don't you think you should finish getting
ready?

RUTH:

Finish? This is it!

TILLIE:

Are you going to wear that sweater?

RUTH:

Look, don't worry about me. I'm not getting
up on any stage, and if I did I wouldn't be
caught dead with a horrible bow like that.

TILLIE:

Mother put it—

RUTH:

They're going to laugh you off the stage again
like when you cranked that atom in assembly . . .
I didn't mean that . . . The one they're going
to laugh at is Mama.

TILLIE:

What?

RUTH:

I said the one they're going to laugh at is

Mama . . . Oh, let me take that bow off.

TILLIE:

It's all right.

RUTH:

Look, just sit still. I don't want everybody making fun of you.

TILLIE:

What made you say that about Mama?

RUTH:

Oh, I heard them talking in the Science Office yesterday. Mr. Goodman and Miss Hanley. She's getting $12.63 to chaperon the thing tonight.

TILLIE:

What were they saying?

RUTH:

Miss Hanley was telling Mr. Goodman about Mama . . . when she found out you were one of the five winners. And he wanted to know if there was something wrong with Mama because she sounded crazy over the phone. And Miss Hanley said she was crazy and she always has been crazy and she can't wait to see what she looks like after all these years.

Miss Hanley said her nickname used to be *Betty the Loon.*

TILLIE: *As* RUTH *combs her hair.*
Ruth, you're hurting me.

RUTH:
She was just like you and everybody thought she was a big weirdo. There! You look much better!

She goes back to the rabbit.

Peter, if anybody stuck you in a pot of boiling water I'd kill them, do you know that? . . .

Then to TILLIE.

What do they call boiling the skin off a cat? I call it murder, that's what I call it. They say it was hit by a car and Janice just scooped it up and before you could say *bingo* it was screaming in a pot of boiling water . . .

Do you know what they're all waiting to see? Mama's feathers! That's what Miss Hanley said. She said Mama blabs as though she was the Queen of England and just as proper as can be, and that her idea of getting dressed up is to put on all the feathers in the world and go as a bird. Always trying to get somewhere, like a great big bird.

TILLIE:

Don't tell Mama, please. It doesn't matter.

RUTH:

I was up there watching her getting dressed and sure enough, she's got the feathers out.

TILLIE:

You didn't tell her what Miss Hanley said?

RUTH:

Are you kidding? I just told her I didn't like the feathers and I didn't think she should wear any. But I'll bet she doesn't listen to me.

TILLIE:

It doesn't matter.

RUTH:

It doesn't matter? Do you think I want to be laughed right out of the school tonight, with

Chris Burns there, and all? Laughed right out of the school, with your electric hair and her feathers on that stage, and Miss Hanley splitting her sides?

TILLIE:
Promise me you won't say anything.

RUTH:
On one condition.

TILLIE:
What?

RUTH:
Give Peter to me.

TILLIE: *Ignoring her.*
The taxi will be here any minute and I won't have all this stuff ready. Did you see my speech?

RUTH:
I mean it. Give Peter to me.

TILLIE:
He belongs to all of us.

RUTH:

For me. All for me. What do you care? He doesn't mean anything to you anymore, now that you've got all those crazy plants.

TILLIE:

Will you stop?

RUTH:

If you don't give him to me I'm going to tell Mama that everybody's waiting to laugh at her.

TILLIE:

Where are those typewritten cards?

RUTH:

I MEAN IT! Give him to me!

TILLIE:

Does he mean that much to you?

RUTH:

Yes!

TILLIE:

All right.

RUTH: *After a burst of private laughter.*
Betty the Loon . . .

She laughs again.

That's what they used to call her, you know.
Betty the Loon!

TILLIE:
I don't think that's very nice.

RUTH:
First they had Betty the Loon, and now
they've got Tillie the Loon . . .

To rabbit.

You don't have to worry about me turning you
in for any old plants . . .

How much does a taxi cost from here to the
school?

TILLIE:
Not much.

RUTH:

I wish she'd give me the money it costs for a taxi—and for all that cardboard and paint and flowerpots and stuff. The only time she ever made a fuss over me was when she drove me nuts.

TILLIE:

Tell her to hurry, please.

RUTH:

By the way, I went over to see Janice Vickery's pot, that she did you know what in, and I started telling her and her mother about the worms in Mr. Alexander Brougham's legs, and I got thrown out because it was too near dinner time. That Mrs. Vickery kills me. She can't stand worms in somebody else's legs but she lets her daughter cook a cat.

TILLIE: *Calling upstairs.*

Mother! The taxi will be here any minute.

BEATRICE *comes to the top of the stairs. Her costume is strange, but not that strange, by any means. She is even a little attractive tonight, and though her words say she is greatly annoyed with*

*having to attend the night's function, her tone and
direction show she is very, very proud.*

BEATRICE:

You're lucky I'm coming, without all this rush-
ing me.

TILLIE:

Mama, you look beautiful.

BEATRICE:

Don't put it on too thick. I said I'd go and I
guess there's no way to get out of it. Do you
mind telling me how I'm supposed to get up
on the stage? Do they call my name or what?
And where are you going to be? If you ask me,
they should've sent all the parents a mimeo-
graphed sheet of instructions. If this is supposed to be such a great event, why don't they
do it right?

TILLIE:

You just sit on the stage with the other parents
before it begins.

BEATRICE:

How long is this thing going to last? And
remember, I don't care even if you do win the

whole damn thing, I'm not making any speech. I can hold my own anywhere, but I hated that school when I went there and I hate it now . . . and the only thing I'd have to say is, what a pack of stupid teachers and vicious children they have. Imagine someone tearing the skin off a cat.

RUTH:
She didn't tear it. She boiled it off.

BEATRICE:
You just told me upstairs that girl tore the skin off with an orange knife and . . . do you know, sometimes you exasperate me?

To TILLIE.

If you've got all the plants in this box, I can manage the folding thing. Do you know I've got a headache from doing those titles? And you probably don't even like them.

TILLIE:
I like them very much.

BEATRICE:
Look, if you don't want me to go tonight, I

don't have to. You're about as enthusiastic as a dummy about this whole thing.

TILLIE:
I'm sorry.

BEATRICE:
And I refuse to let you get nervous. Put that bow back in your hair.

RUTH:
I took it out.

BEATRICE:
What did you do that for?

RUTH: *Taking the rabbit in her arms*.
Because it made her look crazy.

BEATRICE:
How would you know what's crazy or not? If that sweater of yours was any tighter it'd cut off the circulation in your chest.

Fussing over TILLIE.

The bow looks very nice in your hair. There's nothing wrong with looking proper, Matilda, and if you don't have enough money to look expensive and perfect, people like you for *trying* to look nice. You know, one day maybe you will be pretty. You'll have some nice features, when that hair revives and you do some tricks with makeup. I hope you didn't crowd the plants too close together. Did you find your speech?

TILLIE:
Yes, Mother.

BEATRICE:
You know, Matilda, I was wondering about something. Do you think you're really going to win? I mean, not that you won't be the best, but there's so much politics in school. Don't laugh, but if there's anyone who's an expert on that, it's me, and someday I'm going to write a book and blast that school to pieces. If you're just a little bit different in this world, they try to kill you off.

RUTH: *Putting on her coat.*
Tillie gave Peter to me.

BEATRICE:
Oh? Then you inherited the rabbit droppings

I found upstairs. What are you doing with your coat on?

RUTH:

I'm going out to wait for the taxi.

BEATRICE:

Oh, no you're not. You start right in on the rabbit droppings. Or you won't get another cigarette even if you scratch my back with an orange knife.

RUTH:

I'm going down to the school with you.

BEATRICE:

Oh, no you're not! You're going to keep company with that corpse in there. If she wakes up and starts gagging just slip her a shot of whiskey.

The taxi horn blows outside.

Quick! Grab the plants, Matilda—I'll get the big thing.

RUTH:

I want to go! I promised Chris Burns I'd meet him.

BEATRICE:
>Can't you understand English?

RUTH:
>I've got to go!

BEATRICE:
>Shut up!

RUTH: *Almost berserk.*
>I don't care. I'M GOING ANYWAY!

BEATRICE: *Shoving* RUTH *hard.*
>WHAT DID YOU SAY?

TILLIE:
>Mother!

After a pause, the horn blows again.

BEATRICE:
>Hurry up with that box, Matilda, and tell him to stop blowing the horn. HURRY UP!

TILLIE *reluctantly exits with the box of plants.*

>I don't know where you ever got the idea you were going tonight. Did you think nobody was going to hold down the fort? . . .

Now you know how I felt all those years you and everybody else was running out whenever they felt like it—because there was always me to watch over the fifty-dollar-a-week corpse. If there's one thing I demand it's respect. I don't ask for anything from you but respect.

RUTH: *Pathetically.*
Why are you ashamed of me?

BEATRICE:
I've been seen with a lot worse than you. I don't even know why I'm going tonight, do you know that? Do you think I give one goddam about the whole thing? . . .

She starts to fold the large three-panel screen with the titles: THE PAST, THE PRESENT, *and* THE FUTURE.

Do you want to know why I'm going? Do you really want to know why this once somebody else has to stick with that dried prune for a few minutes? Because this is the first time in my life I've ever felt just a little bit proud over something. Isn't that silly? Somewhere in the back of this turtle-sized brain of mine I feel just a little *proud*! Jesus Christ! And you begrudge me even that, you little bastard.

The taxi horn blows impatiently.

RUTH: *In a hard voice.*
Hurry up. They're waiting for you . . . They're *all* waiting for you.

BEATRICE: *Carrying the folded screen so that* THE PAST *is face out in bold black letters.*
I hope the paint is dry . . . Who's waiting for me?

RUTH:
Everybody . . . including Miss Hanley. She's been telling all the teachers . . . about you . . . and they're all waiting.

BEATRICE:
You're such a little liar, Ruth, do you know that? When you can't have what you want, you try to ruin it for everybody else.

She starts to the door.

RUTH:
Goodnight, *Betty the Loon.*

BEATRICE *stops as if she's been stabbed.*

The taxi horn blows several times as BEATRICE *puts down the folding screen.*

BEATRICE: *Helplessly.*
Take this thing.

RUTH:
What for?

BEATRICE:
Go with Matilda.

RUTH:
I don't want to go now.

BEATRICE: *Blasting.*
GET OUT OF HERE!

RUTH: *After a long pause.*
Now Tillie's going to blame it on me that you're not going—and take the rabbit back.

The taxi beeps again, as RUTH *puts her coat on.*

I can't help it what people call you.

She picks up the screen.

I'll tell Tillie you'll be down later, all right? . . .

Don't answer me. What do I care!

RUTH *exits.*

BEATRICE *breaks into tears that shudder her body, and the lights go down slowly on her pathetic form. Music in.*

*Suddenly a bolt of light strikes an area in the right stage—*JANICE VICKERY *is standing in the spotlight holding the skeleton of a cat mounted on a small platform. Her face and voice are smug.*

JANICE:
The Past: I got the cat from the A.S.P.C.A. immediately after it had been killed by a high-altitude pressure system. That explains why some of the rib bones are missing, because that method sucks the air out of the animal's lungs and ruptures all cavities. They say it prevents cruelty to animals but I think it's horrible.

She laughs.

Then I boiled the cat in a sodium hydroxide solution until most of the skin pulled right off, but I had to scrape some of the grizzle off the joints with a knife. You have no idea how difficult it is to get right down to the bones.

A little gong sounds.

I have to go on to *The Present*, now—but I did want to tell you how long it took me to put the thing together. I mean, as it is now, it's extremely useful for students of anatomy, even with the missing rib bones, and it can be used to show basic anatomical aspects of many, many animals that are in the same family as felines. I suppose that's about the only present uses I can think for it, but it is nice to remember as an accomplishment, and it looks good on college applications to show you did something else in school besides dating.

She laughs, and a second gong sounds.

The Future: The only future plans I have for Tabby—my little brother asked the A.S.P.C.A. what its name was when he went to pick it up and they said it was called Tabby, but I think they were kidding him—

She laughs again.

I mean as far as future plans, I'm going to donate it to the science department, of course, and next year, if there's another Science Fair perhaps I'll do the same thing with a dog.

A third gong sounds.

Thank you very much for your attention, and I hope I win!

JANICE *and her spotlight disappear as suddenly as they had arrived, and music returns as the lights come up slowly on* BEATRICE.

She has obviously been drinking and is going through a phone book. Finding her number, she goes to the phone and dials.

BEATRICE: *Into the phone.*
I want to talk to the principal, please . . .

Well, you'll have to get him down off the stage . . .

It's none of your goddam business who I am! . . .

Oh, I see . . . Yes. I have a message for him and Mr. Goodman, and you, too . . . And this is for Miss Hanley, too . . .

Tell them Mrs. Hunsdorfer called to thank them for making her wish she was dead . . . Would you give them that message, please? . . . Thank you very much.

She hangs up the phone, pauses, then surveys the room. Her attention fixes on the store window covered with newspapers. The phone rings several times but she ignores it. She goes to the window and proceeds to rip the paper from it. That finished, she turns and surveys the room again. She goes to the kitchen table and rearranges its position. She spies a card table with school supplies and hurls them on the floor. Next, she goes to a bureau and rummages through drawers, finding tablecloths and napkins. She throws cloths on two or three tables and is heading toward the kitchen table when the phone rings again. The ringing triggers off something else she wants to do. She empties a cup filled with scraps of paper and finds a telephone number. She lifts the receiver off the ringing phone and hangs up immediately. She lifts the receiver again, checks to make sure there's a dial tone, and then dials the number on the scrap of paper.

BEATRICE: *Into the phone.*

Hello. This is Mrs. Hunsdorfer . . . I'm sorry if I frightened you, I wouldn't want you to think Nanny had deceased or anything like that—I can imagine how terrible you'd feel if anything like that ever happened . . . Terrible tragedy that would be, Miss Career Woman of the Year . . .

Yes, I'll tell you why I'm calling. I want her out of here by tomorrow. I told you when you rolled her in here I was going to try her out for a while and if I didn't like her she was to get the hell out. Well I don't like her, so get her the hell out . . .

It's like this. I don't like the way she cheats at solitaire. Is that a good enough reason? . . . Fine. And if she's not out of here by noon I'll send her collect in an ambulance, you son of a bitch!

She slams down the phone and bursts into laughter. The laughter subsides somewhat as she pours herself another drink. She takes the drink to a chair and as she sits down her foot accidentally hits the rabbit cage. She gives the cage a little kick and then an idea strikes. She gets up and finds a large blue towel which she flings over her shoulder. She gets the bottle of chloroform and approaches the cage. Having reached a decision she picks up the cage and takes it upstairs.

Music in and lights fade.

From the darkness a beam of light falls on TILLIE *in the same way* JANICE VICKERY *had been presented.*

TILLIE: *Deathly afraid, and referring to her cards.*
The Past: The seeds were exposed to various degrees . . . of gamma rays from radiation sources in Oak Ridge . . .

Mr. Goodman helped me pay for the seeds . . . Their growth was plotted against . . . time.

She loses her voice for a moment and then the first gong sounds.

The Present: The seeds which received little radiation have grown to plants which are normal in appearance. The seeds which received moderate radiation gave rise to mutations such as double blooms, giant stems, and variegated leaves. The seeds closest to the gamma source were killed or yielded dwarf plants.

The second gong rings.

The Future: After radiation is better understood, a day will come when the power from exploding atoms will change the whole world we know.

With inspiration.

Some of the mutations will be good ones—wonderful things beyond our dreams—and I believe, I believe this with all my heart, THE DAY WILL COME WHEN MANKIND WILL THANK GOD FOR THE STRANGE AND BEAUTIFUL ENERGY FROM THE ATOM.

Part of her last speech is reverberated electronically. Deep pulses of music are added as the light focuses on TILLIE'*s face.*

Suddenly there is silence, except for RUTH *picking up* TILLIE'*s last words.*

The lights come up on the main set, and the room is empty.

RUTH *bursts in the front door. She is carrying the three-panel card and a shopping bag of plants, both of which she drops on the floor.*

RUTH:
MAMA! MAMA! She won! Mama! Where are you? She won!

She runs back to the front door and yells to TILLIE.

Hurry up! Hurry! Oh, my God, I can't believe it!

Then yelling upstairs.

Mama! Come on down! Hurry!

TILLIE *comes in the front door, carrying the rest of her plants, and the large trophy.*

RUTH *takes the trophy.*

Give me that!

She starts upstairs.

Mama! Wait till you see this!

BEATRICE *appears at the top of the stairs. She has been drinking a great deal, and clings fast to a bunch of old cheap curtains and other material.*

Mama! She won . . .

BEATRICE *continues mechanically on down the stairs.*

Didn't you hear me? Tillie won the whole thing! . . . Mama? . . . What's the matter with you? What did you rip the paper off the windows for?

BEATRICE *commences tacking up one of the curtains.*

TILLIE:
Mama? Are you going to open a . . . shop?

RUTH:
What's the matter? Can't you even answer?

BEATRICE: *To* TILLIE.
Hand me some of those tacks.

RUTH: *Screaming*.
　　I SAID SHE WON! ARE YOU DEAF?

BEATRICE:
　　Ruth, if you don't shut up I'm going to have
　　you put away.

RUTH:
　　They ought to put *you* away, BETTY THE
　　LOON!

　　There is a long pause.

BEATRICE:
　　The rabbit is in your room. I want you to bury
　　it in the morning.

RUTH:
　　If you did anything . . . I'LL KILL YOU!

　　She runs upstairs.

TILLIE:
　　Mother, you didn't kill it, did you?

BEATRICE:
　　Nanny goes tomorrow. First thing tomorrow.

There is a cry from upstairs.

TILLIE:
Ruth? Are you all right?

BEATRICE:
I don't know what it's going to be. Maybe a tea shop. Maybe not.

RUTH *appears in the doorway of her room. She is holding the dead rabbit on the blue towel. As she reaches the top of the stairs, she begins to moan deeply.*

After school you're going to have regular hours. You'll work in the kitchen, you'll learn how to cook, and you're going to earn your keep, just like in any other business.

TILLIE *starts slowly up the stairs toward* RUTH.

TILLIE: *With great fear.*
Mama . . . I think she's *going to go.*

RUTH *commences to tremble.* TILLIE *speaks softly to her.*

Don't go . . . don't go . . .

RUTH's *eyes roll in her head, and the trembling of her body becomes pronounced throbbing. She drops the rabbit with the towel covering it.*

Help me! Mama! Help me!

BEATRICE:
Snap out of it, do you hear me? RUTH, DON'T LET YOURSELF GO!

To TILLIE.

Help me get her downstairs!

By the time the trio reaches the bottom of the stairs, RUTH *is consumed by a violent convulsion.* BEATRICE *holds her down and pushes* TILLIE *out of the way.*

BEATRICE: *Screaming.*
Get the wooden spoon!

TILLIE *responds as* BEATRICE *gets* RUTH *onto a sofa. The convulsion runs its course of a full minute, then finally subsides.* TILLIE *gets a blanket and covers* RUTH.

TILLIE:
> Shall I call the doctor?

> *There is a long pause.*

> Shall I call the doctor?

BEATRICE:
> No. She'll be all right.

TILLIE:
> I think we should call him.

BEATRICE:
> I DIDN'T ASK YOU WHAT YOU THOUGHT! . . . We're going to need every penny to get this place open.

> BEATRICE *spreads a tablecloth on one of the tables and places a pile of old cloth napkins on it. She sits down and lights a cigarette.*

TILLIE: *Picking up the rabbit on the stairs.*
> I'd better bury him in the backyard.

> *She starts out.*

BEATRICE:
 Don't bury the towel.

 TILLIE stops, sobs audibly, then gets control.

TILLIE:
 I'll do it in the morning.

 She gently lays the rabbit near the door. She tucks RUTH *in on the couch and sits a few minutes by her sleeping sister.*

 Music starts in softly as BEATRICE *continues folding napkins with her back to the others.*

 There is the sound of someone at the curtained doorway, and NANNY *commences negotiating herself into the room. Slowly she advances with the tubular frame—unaware, desiccated, in some other land.*

BEATRICE: *Weakly.*
 Matilda?

TILLIE:
 Yes, Mama?

BEATRICE:
I hate the world. Do you know that, Matilda?

TILLIE:
Yes, Mama.

BEATRICE:
I hate the world.

The lights have started down, the music makes its presence known, and a spot clings to TILLIE. *She moves to the staircase and the rest of the set goes to black during the following speech. As she starts up the stairs her recorded voice takes over as in the opening of the play.*

TILLIE'S VOICE:
The Conclusion: My experiment has shown some of the strange effects radiation can produce . . . and how dangerous it can be if not handled correctly.

Mr. Goodman said I should tell in this conclusion what my future plans are and how this experiment has helped me make them.

For one thing, the effect of gamma rays on

man-in-the-moon marigolds has made me curious about the sun and the stars, for the universe itself must be like a world of great atoms—and I want to know more about it. But most important, I suppose, my experiment has made me feel important—every atom in me, in everybody, has come from the sun—from places beyond our dreams. The atoms of our hands, the atoms of our hearts . . .

All sound out.

TILLIE *speaks the rest live—hopeful, glowing.*

Atom.
Atom.
What a beautiful word.

THE END